HOPSCOTCH ADVENTURES

Sinbad and the Whale

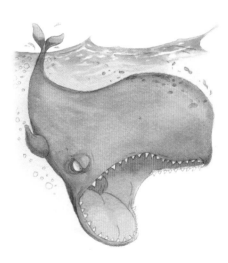

by Martin Waddell and O'Kif

W
FRANKLIN WATTS
LONDON•SYDNEY

First published in 2009 by
Franklin Watts
338 Euston Road
London
NW1 3BH

Franklin Watts Australia
Level 17/207 Kent Street
Sydney
NSW 2000

A CIP catalogue record for this book is available
from the British Library.

ISBN 978 0 7496 8553 9 (hbk)
ISBN 978 0 7496 8565 2 (pbk)

Series Editor: Jackie Hamley
Series Advisor: Dr Barrie Wade
Series Designer: Peter Scoulding

Printed in China

Franklin Watts is a division of
Hachette Children's Books,
an Hachette UK company
www.hachette.co.uk

ARABIA

DUDLEY SCHOOLS
LIBRARY SERVICE

Sinbad the Sailor made pots of
money on his first voyage to sea.

On the way home, his ship sailed by a low-lying, beautiful island.

"Yippee!" cheered the crew
as they landed.

"We'll hold a We're-Rich-Now party in honour of Sinbad the Sailor."

Sinbad felt uneasy. "There's something fishy about this place!" he warned his friend Ali.

Ali was too busy to listen.

He lit the fire for the barbecue

and...

...the island woke up! It lashed its huge tail, and it **moved!**

"Oh no!" gasped Sinbad.

"This island's a whale!"

WOOOOOOOOSH!

They all ended up in the sea.

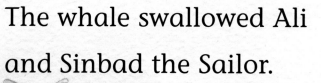

The whale swallowed Ali
and Sinbad the Sailor.

14

The rest of the crew swam back to
the ship and sailed sadly home.

Deep, deep down inside the
whale, Ali and Sinbad were
swimming in smelly water.
There were small crabs and huge
jellyfish and broken palm trees.
"How do we get out of this?"
groaned Ali.

"Think, think, THINK!" Sinbad
said. And he thought...

And he thought...

"It's whale tickle time!"
laughed Sinbad.

Sinbad grabbed a palm tree,
stripped off the palms and
handed Ali the trunk.

"Swim back up to the mouth and
wait by the teeth," Sinbad told Ali.
Then Sinbad swam to the whale's
throat.

He tickled and tickled and tickled
until the whale started to cough.

YARRRGGGHHH!

"NOW!" yelled Sinbad.

"Here we go!"

WOOOOOOOOSH!

They were out of the whale, but lost at sea, bobbing about on a broken palm tree! "What now?" sighed Ali.

"Leave it to me!" said Sinbad.
He knew how to steer by the
stars so they set off for home.

The palm tree sailed into the harbour. The ship was there with all Sinbad's pots full of money.

"You're back!" cried the crew.

"We thought we'd lost you!"

Then Sinbad, Ali and the crew
had their We're-Rich-Now party...
but not on the whale!

Puzzle 1

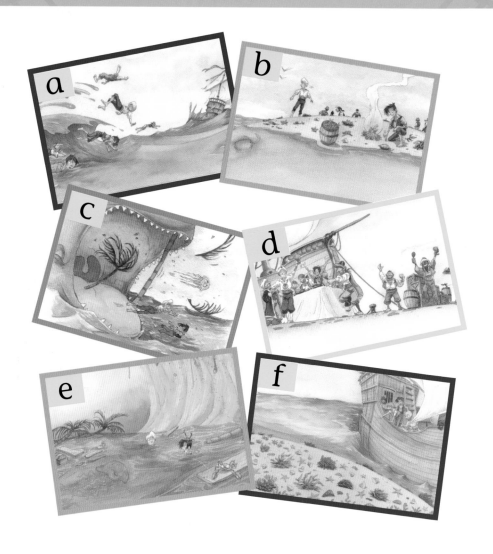

Put these pictures in the correct order.
Which event do you think is most important?
Now try writing the story in your own words!

Puzzle 2

1. There's a crab on my head!

2. I'll tickle the whale's throat!

3. Let's have a party!

4. How will we ever find dry land?

5. Can anyone see them?

6. I have a bad feeling about this island.

Choose the correct speech bubbles for the characters above. Can you think of any others? Turn over to find the answers.

Answers

Puzzle 1

The correct order is: 1f, 2b, 3a, 4e, 5c, 6d

Puzzle 2

Ali: 1, 4

Sinbad: 2, 6

The crew: 3, 5

Look out for more Hopscotch Adventures:

TALES OF KING ARTHUR

1. The Sword in the Stone
ISBN 978 0 7496 6694 1

2. Arthur the King
ISBN 978 0 7496 6695 8

3. The Round Table
ISBN 978 0 7496 6697 2

4. Sir Lancelot and the Ice Castle
ISBN 978 0 7496 6698 9

5. Sir Gawain and the Green Knight
ISBN 978 0 7496 8557 7*
ISBN 978 0 7496 8569 0

6. Sir Galahad and the Holy Grail
ISBN 978 0 7496 8558 4*
ISBN 978 0 7496 8570 6

TALES OF ROBIN HOOD

Robin and the Knight
ISBN 978 0 7496 6699 6

Robin and the Monk
ISBN 978 0 7496 6700 9

Robin and the Silver Arrow
ISBN 978 0 7496 6703 0

Robin and the Friar
ISBN 978 0 7496 6702 3

Robin and the Butcher
ISBN 978 0 7496 8555 3*
ISBN 978 0 7496 8568 3

Robin and Maid Marian
ISBN 978 0 7496 8556 0*
ISBN 978 0 7496 8567 6

TALES OF SINBAD THE SAILOR

Sinbad and the Ogre
ISBN 978 0 7496 8559 1*
ISBN 978 0 7496 8571 3

Sinbad and the Whale
ISBN 978 0 7496 8553 9*
ISBN 978 0 7496 8565 2

Sinbad and the Diamond Valley
ISBN 978 0 7496 8554 6*
ISBN 978 0 7496 8566 9

Sinbad and the Monkeys
ISBN 978 0 7496 8560 7*
ISBN 978 0 7496 8572 0

For more *Hopscotch Adventures* and other *Hopscotch* stories, visit:
www.franklinwatts.co.uk

* hardback